MARVEL
SPIDEY
and his AMAZING FRIENDS

Construction Destruction

Adapted by **Steve Behling**
Based on the episode written by **Sib Ventress**
Illustrated by **Premise Entertainment**

MARVEL

Los Angeles • New York

SUSTAINABLE
FORESTRY
INITIATIVE

Certified Chain of Custody
Promoting Sustainable Forestry

www.sfiprogram.org
SFI-01415

The SFI label applies to the text stock

What started as a quiet day for **Spidey** has become very busy! A Spidey-alert sends Peter Parker scrambling for his Super Hero costume. Then he heads for the WEB-Quarters to see what the problem is.

"Spidey!" **Ms. Marvel** says over the viewscreen. "I'm with **Hulk**, and we need your help!"

"Ms. Marvel? And Hulk?" Spidey says. "This must be **big**!"

Spidey hears a **loud crashing** sound behind Ms. Marvel as she sends her location to him.

As Spidey gets ready to leave, Hulk pushes his face right up in front of the camera.

"Please hurry!" Hulk shouts.

The image on the viewscreen shakes and then goes black.

"I've sent the location to your **Web-Crawler**," says WEB-STER, the computer in the WEB-Quarters.

Spidey doesn't waste a second. He hops into the Web-Crawler and starts the engine.

"Time to web-out!" he says.

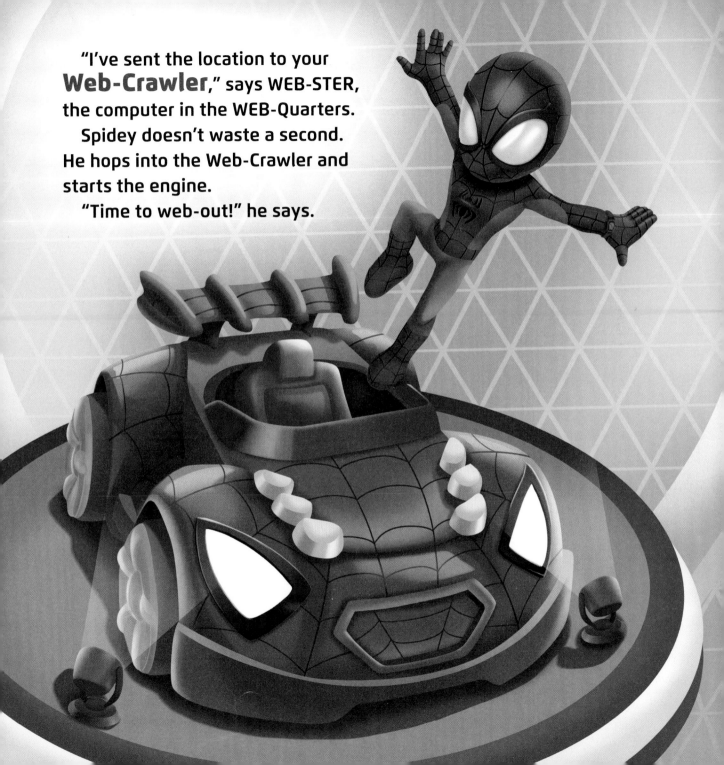

Only a few seconds pass before the Web-Crawler **zooms** onto the city streets! Spidey is sure this must be a **big emergency** for both Ms. Marvel and Hulk to need his help.

Like a race-car driver, Spidey guides the Web-Crawler toward his destination.

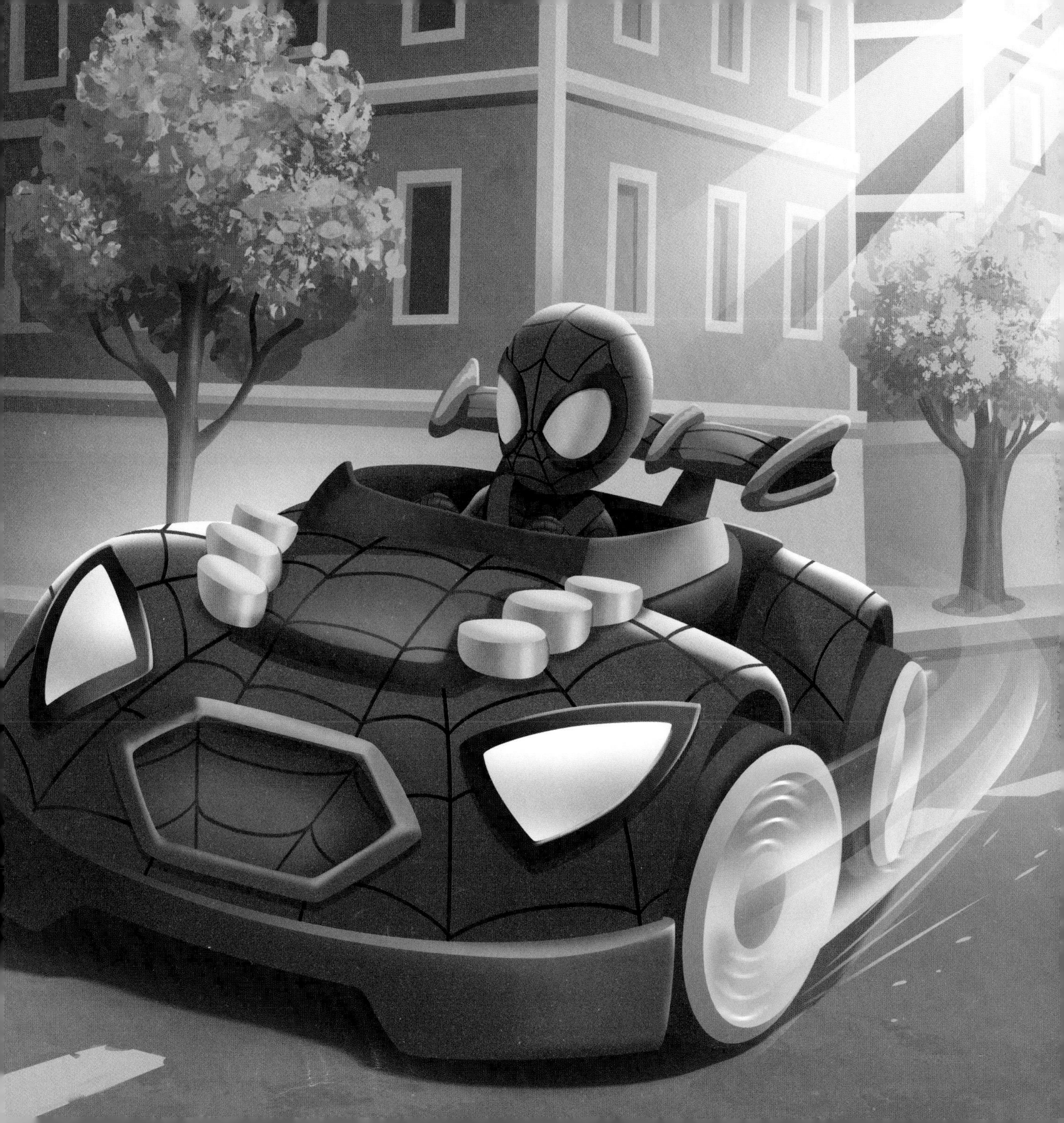

Minutes later, Spidey arrives at a construction site. He sees a large wooden house frame. Ms. Marvel's Embiggen Bike and Hulk's Smash Truck are parked outside. Spidey pulls up and hops out of the Web-Crawler.

"Ms. Marvel! Hulk!" Spidey calls out as he sees Ms. Marvel and Hulk standing next to a construction worker. "I got here as fast as I could! What's the emergency?"

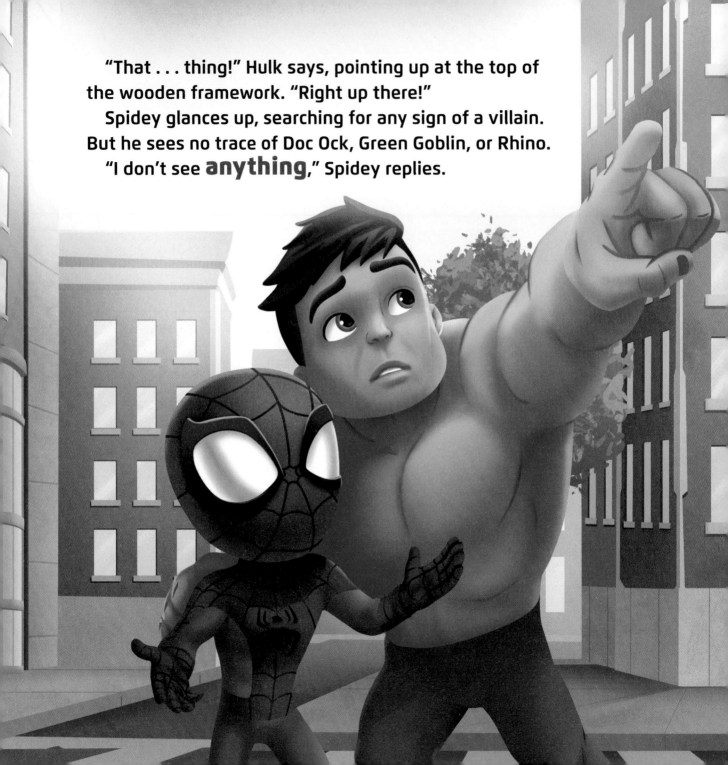

"That . . . thing!" Hulk says, pointing up at the top of the wooden framework. "Right up there!"

Spidey glances up, searching for any sign of a villain. But he sees no trace of Doc Ock, Green Goblin, or Rhino.

"I don't see **anything**," Spidey replies.

"Oh, none of us saw him at first," the construction worker says.
"He's **sneaky**!"

"And way more **dangerous** than he looks!" Ms. Marvel adds.

"That sounds serious!" Spidey says, but he still can't see anything.

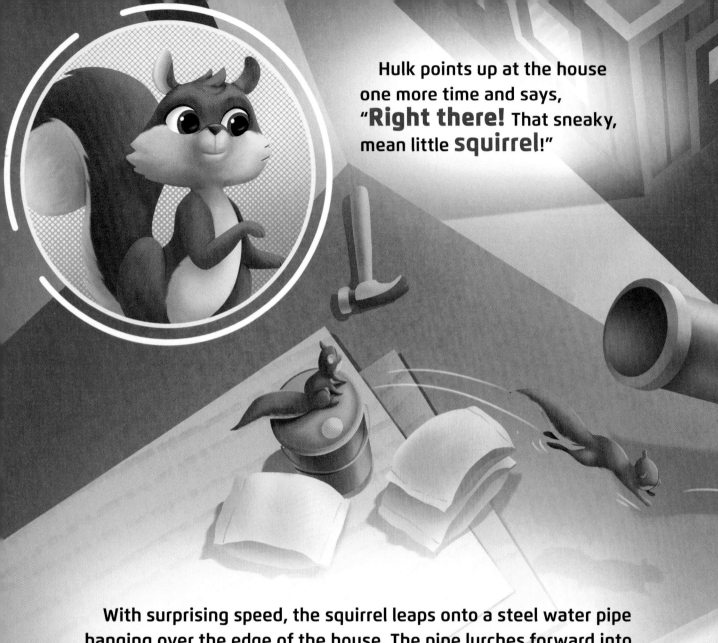

Hulk points up at the house one more time and says, **"Right there!** That sneaky, mean little **squirrel!"**

With surprising speed, the squirrel leaps onto a steel water pipe hanging over the edge of the house. The pipe lurches forward into the air, then falls to the ground with a loud **CLANG!** Meanwhile, the squirrel scampers away on a rope.

"I guess when you called for my help, I thought it would be something . . . **bigger**," Spidey says.

"Oh, that squirrel is a big, big problem, all right," the construction worker moans.

"We've been trying to catch him," Hulk says. "But he's so quick and tricky!"

"He threw acorns at me!" Ms. Marvel complains. "Pointy little acorns!"

Suddenly, Spidey's Spidey-sense goes wild, and a **wooden beam** flies right past him!

"Whoa, look out!" he warns.

The beam smacks right into Hulk's **Smash Truck**.
"He hit my truck!" Hulk says.
Then he starts to get **mad**!
"Take a deep breath, big guy," Ms. Marvel says, and
Hulk calms down.

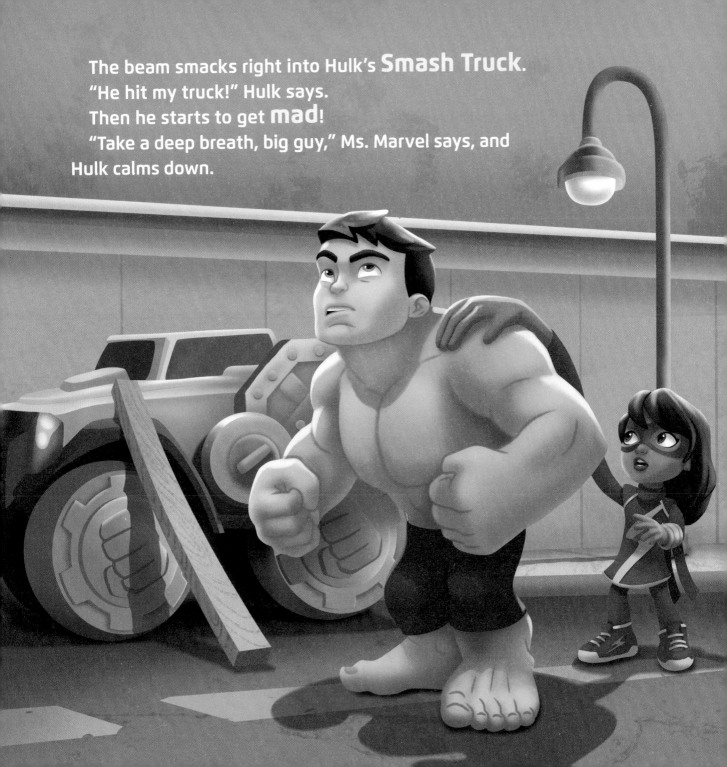

"I've **never** seen a squirrel act like this before," Spidey says.
Spidey swings up to the third floor of the house, where he spies the little squirrel.

"Aha!" Spidey says as he **thwips** a web. "Go-webs-go!"

But the squirrel is **too quick**. It dashes out of the way, and the web hits something else.

When Spidey pulls the web back, he doesn't see the squirrel.

"Somehow, I caught a hammer, not a squirrel!" he says, confused.

But Spidey doesn't give up easily. He goes after the squirrel again. This time, he sees the furry critter sitting on top of the unfinished roof.

Spidey follows the squirrel and calls out, "I'm just trying to help, little guy. Construction sites are **dangerous**. You don't want to get hurt."

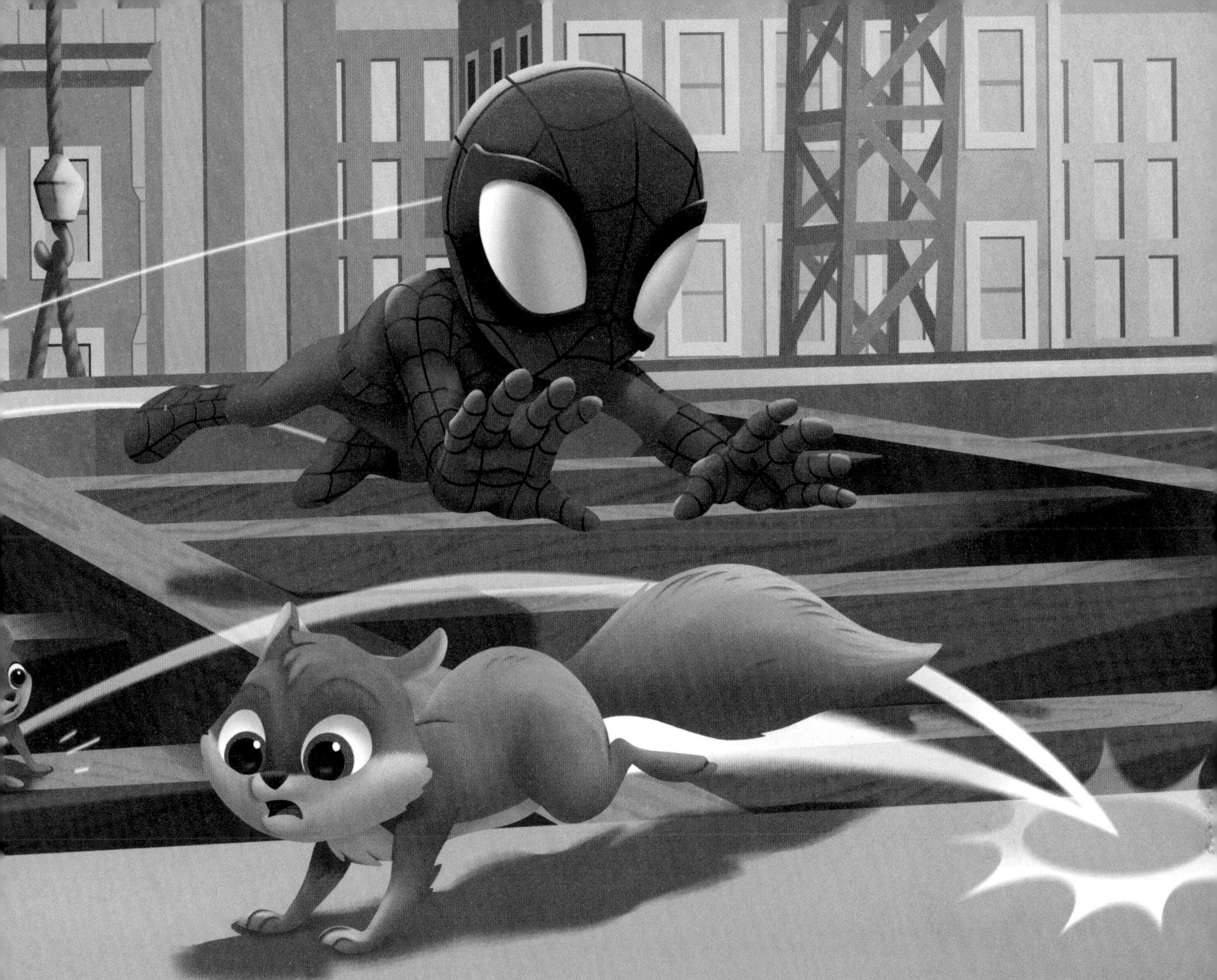

He hops toward the squirrel, but the animal jumps to another wooden beam. So Spidey leaps again. The squirrel continues to run! No matter how fast Spidey jumps, the squirrel is **faster**.

Spidey keeps chasing the squirrel, and Hulk and Ms. Marvel join in. But none of them can come close to catching the animal.

Then the squirrel escapes by jumping into the driver's seat of Hulk's Smash Truck. The weight of the squirrel accidentally starts the engine!

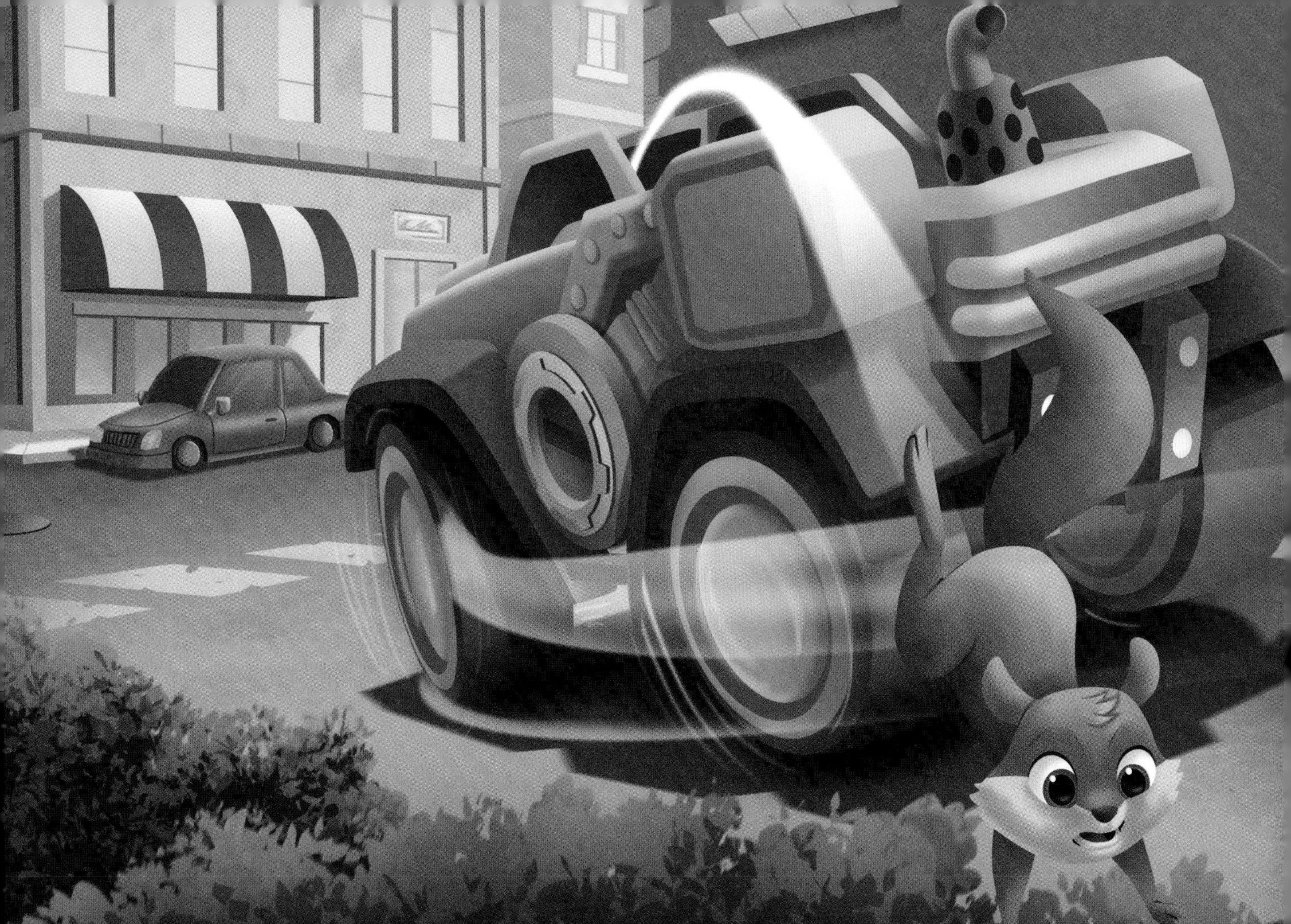

"Uh, Hulk?" Spidey says. "Can you stop your truck?"

"I sure can!" Hulk says.

But the Smash Truck rolls out into the street before Hulk can stop it. The frightened squirrel leaps out of the vehicle and into some bushes.

"Oh, no," Ms. Marvel says. "It's gonna hit that parked car!"

Hulk **speeds** down the street and jumps in front of the Smash Truck. He tries to stop the vehicle, but he **slides on the gravel**! Ms. Marvel helps him, but the truck is still heading for the parked car.

Then Spidey gets an idea. He leaps on top of the Smash Truck and webs the controls.

Spidey pulls on the web, turning off the Smash Truck and it finally stops!

Spidey, Hulk, and Ms. Marvel head back to the construction site. But the squirrel has returned!

The construction worker says all the trouble began when they tried to **cut down a tree** to make room for a driveway.

"That's it!" Spidey says. "This has just been one giant misunderstanding. The squirrel isn't being mean. He's just trying to protect his home."

That gives the heroes a **big idea**. They get permission from the city to move the tree! Hulk uses his incredible strength to carry the tree from the construction site to a nice spot in the park.

With Ms. Marvel's help, Hulk replants the tree where it will keep growing.

"I hope we don't have to outsmart a squirrel again," Ms. Marvel says.

Hulk shudders and says, "Doc Ock, Green Goblin, Rhino . . . I'll help you catch them any day. But no more squirrels!"